THIS WALKER BOOK BELONGS TO: 18

_____

_____

_____

_____

There are days when Bartholomew is naughty,
and other days when he is very very good.

'First published 1997 by Walker Books Ltd, 87 Vauxhall Walk, London SE11 5HJ

This edition published 1999

Reprinted 1999 (twice)

© 1997 Virginia Miller

This book has been typeset in Garamond.

Printed in Hong Kong

British Library Cataloguing in Publication Data
A catalogue record for this book is available from the British Library.

ISBN 0-7445-6329-1

BE GENTLE!

Virginia Miller

WALKER BOOKS
AND SUBSIDIARIES
LONDON • BOSTON • SYDNEY

One day George gave
Bartholomew a little black kitten.
"She's yours to look after," he said. "I'll help,
but be gentle because she's only little."

Bartholomew stroked the little black kitten,
picked her up and gave her a hug.

"Be gentle," George said, "you're squashing her."
"Nah!" said Bartholomew. And he went outside.

He gave the little black kitten a swing,

a ride in his red cart …

then he gave the little black kitten

a surprise with the garden hose.

"No, don't do that," George said.
"Be gentle with her. She's only little
and she doesn't like getting wet."
"Nah!" said Bartholomew.

Bartholomew went inside and played his drum

to cheer up the little black kitten.

"BE GENTLE!"

George said in a big voice.
Bartholomew dropped the little black kitten.

"She's only little, Ba," George said, "and all that noise you've been making has frightened her, and now she's run away."

Bartholomew and George looked and looked,

but they couldn't find the little black kitten.

Bartholomew felt sad and sorry.

He went to sit in his secret hiding place …

where he found

the little black kitten.

The little black kitten sat on his lap.
Bartholomew was very, *very* gentle,
and the little black kitten purred.

MORE WALKER PAPERBACKS
For You to Enjoy

Some more Bartholomew stories by Virginia Miller

ON YOUR POTTY!
George tries to get Bartholomew to use his potty.

"Virginia Miller's drawings of Bartholomew bear are adorably cute."
Baby Magazine

0-7445-3141-1   £4.99

EAT YOUR DINNER!
Bartholomew refuses to eat his dinner – but George has a delicious
honey cake that just might change his mind!

"The illustrations are delightful and bring about instant wry recognition.
A 'must' for any nursery." *Books for Keeps*

0-7445-3154-3   £4.99

GET INTO BED!
It's Bartholomew's bedtime. But Bartholomew doesn't want to go to bed.
Will George ever get him to fall asleep?

"Wins my commendation as the cuddliest of the season's publications.
Bartholomew is a beautifully observed toddler."
Wendy Cope, The Daily Telegraph

0-7445-3629-4   £4.99